SCHALKEN THE PAINTER

BY

JOSEPH SHERIDAN LE FANU

British Library Cataloguing-in-Publication Data
A catalogue record for this book is available from the
British Library

CONTENTS

JOSEPH SHERIDAN LE FANU

Joseph Thomas Sheridan Le Fanu was born in Dublin in 1814. His was a literary family of Huguenot origins; both his grandmother Alicia Sheridan Le Fanu and his great-uncle Richard Brinsley Sheridan were playwrights, and his niece Rhoda Broughton would go on to become a successful novelist. Le Fanu's family lived in a variety of locations around rural Ireland during his youth—the folk superstitions of which are said to have left a deep impression on him—and were financially hard-hit by the agitations of the Tithe Wars. In 1833, not long after the death of his father, Le Fanu entered Trinity College, Dublin to study law. While there, he was elected Auditor of the College Historical Society, and between 1838 and 1840 published his first series of short stories, which were later collected as *The Purcell Papers*.

Le Fanu was called to the bar in 1839, but he never practiced and soon abandoned law for journalism. During the 1840s, he married, and spent time mounting a protest against the indifference of the government to the Irish Famine. He also produced his first two novels—*The Cock and Anchor* (1845) and *The Fortunes of Colonel Torlogh O'Brien* (1847); both works of historical fiction—and in 1851 he and his wife Susanna moved to their house on Merrion Square, Dublin, where le Fanu was to remain until his death. In 1858, Le Fanu's wife Susanna died in unclear circumstances, and he became a recluse, setting to work in his most productive and successful years as a writer. Between 1864 and 1872, he produced ten novels, all in the 'sensation fiction' genre popular at the time.

At his peak, le Fanu was the leading ghost-story writer of the nineteenth century, and he is now seen as central to the development of the genre in the Victorian era. His work is credited with turning the Gothic's focus from the external sources of horror to the inward effects of terror, thus helping to create the psychological basis for supernaturalist literature that continues to this day. Arguably le Fanu's most enduring works are *Uncle Silas*, published in 1864, and the vampire novella *Camilla* (1872), which influenced Bram Stoker in the writing of *Dracula* and has inspired several films. Le Fanu died in his native Dublin in 1873, at the age of 58.

SCHALKEN THE PAINTER

by Joseph Sheridan Le Fanu

You will no doubt be surprised, my dear friend, at the subject of the following narrative. What had I to do with Schalken, or Schalken with me? He had returned to his native land, and was probably dead and buried before I was born; I never visited Holland nor spoke with a native of that country. So much I believe you already know. I must, then, give you my authority, and state to you frankly the ground upon which rests the credibility of the strange story which I am about to lay before you. I was acquainted, in my early days, with a Captain Vandael, whose father had served King William in the Low Countries, and also in my own unhappy land during the Irish campaigns. I know not how it happened that I liked this man's society in spite of his politics and religion: but so it was; and it was by means of the free intercourse to which our intimacy gave rise that I became possessed of the curious tale which you are about to hear. I had often been struck, while visiting Vandael, by a remarkable picture, in which, though no *connoisseur* myself, I could not fail to discern some very strong peculiarities, particularly in the distribution of light and shade, as also a certain oddity in the design itself, which interested my curiosity. It represented the interior of what might be a chamber in some antique religious building—the foreground was occupied by a female figure, arrayed in a species of white robe, part of which is arranged so as to form a veil. The dress, however, is not strictly that of any religious order. In its hand the figure bears a lamp, by whose light alone the form and face are illuminated; the features are marked by an arch smile, such as pretty women wear when engaged in successfully practising some roguish trick; in the background, and, excepting where the dim red light of an expiring fire serves to define the form, totally in the shade, stands the figure of a man equipped in the old fashion, with doublet and so forth, in an attitude of alarm, his hand being placed upon the hilt of his sword, which he appears to be in the act of drawing.

"There are some pictures," said I to my friend, "which impress one, I know not how, with a conviction that they represent not the mere ideal shapes and combinations which have floated through the imagination of the artist, but scenes, faces, and situations which have actually existed. When I look upon that picture, something assures me that I behold the representation of a reality."

Vandael smiled, and fixing his eyes upon the painting musingly, he said:

"Your fancy has not deceived you, my good friend, for that picture is the record, and I believe a faithful one, of a remarkable and mysterious occurrence. It was painted by Schalken, and contains, in the face of the female figure, which occupies the most prominent place in the design, an accurate portrait of Rose Velderkaust, the niece of Gerard Douw, the first, and, I believe, the only love of Godfrey Schalken. My father knew the painter well and from Schalken himself he learned the story of the mysterious drama, one scene of which the picture has embodied. This painting, which is accounted a fine specimen of Schalken's style, was bequeathed to my father by the artist's will, and, as you have observed, is a very striking and interesting production."

I had only to request Vandael to tell the story of the painting to be gratified; and thus it is that I am enabled to submit to you a faithful recital of what I heard myself, leaving you to reject or allow the evidence upon which the truth of the tradition depends, with this one assurance, that Schalken was an honest, blunt Dutchman, and, I believe, wholly incapable of committing a flight of imagination; and further, that Vandael, from whom I heard the story, appeared firmly convinced of its truth.

There are few forms upon which the mantle of mystery

and romance could seem to hang more ungracefully than upon that of the uncouth and clownish Schalken—the Dutch boor-the rude and dogged, but most cunning worker of oils, whose pieces delight the initiated of the present day almost as much as his manners disgusted the refined of his own; and yet this man, so rude, so dogged, so slovenly, I had almost said so savage, in mien and manner, during his after successes, had been selected by the capricious goddess, in his early life, to figure as the hero of a romance by no means devoid of interest or of mystery. Who can tell how meet he may have been in his young days to play the part of the lover or of the hero—who can say that in early life he had been the same harsh, *unlicked*, and rugged boor which, in his maturer age, he proved-or how far the neglected rudeness which afterwards marked his air and garb, and manners, may not have been the growth of that reckless apathy not unfrequently produced by bitter misfortunes and disappointments in early life? These questions Can never now be answered. We must content ourselves, then, with a plain statement of facts, or what have been received and transmitted as such, leaving matters of speculation to those who like them.

When Schalken studied under the immortal Gerard Douw, he was a young man; and in spite of the phlegmatic constitution and unexcitable manner which he shared (we believe) with his countrymen, he was not incapable of deep and vivid impressions, for it is an established fact that the young painter looked with considerable interest upon the beautiful niece of his wealthy master. Rose Velderkaust was very young, having, at the period of which we speak, not yet attained her seventeenth year, and, if tradition speaks truth, possessed all the soft dimpling charms of the fair, light-haired Flemish maidens. Schalken had not studied long in the school of Gerard Douw, when he felt this interest deepening into something of a keener and intenser feeling that was quite consistent with the tranquillity of his honest Dutch heart; and at the same time he perceived, or thought he perceived, flattering symptoms of a reciprocity of liking, and this was quite sufficient to determine whatever indecision he might have heretofore experienced, and to lead him to devote exclusively to her every hope and feeling of his heart. In short, he was as much in love as a Dutchman could be. He was not long in making his passion known to the pretty maiden herself, and his declaration was followed by a corresponding confession upon her part. Schalken, however, was a poor man, and he possessed no counterbalancing advantages of birth or otherwise to induce the old man to consent to a union which must involve his niece and ward in the struggles and difficulties of a young and nearly friendless artist. He was, therefore, to wait until time had furnished him with opportunity and accident with success; and then, if his labours were found sufficiently lucrative, it was to be hoped that his proposals might at least be listened to by her jealous guardian. Months passed away, and, cheered by the smiles of the little Rose, Schalken's labours were redoubled, and with such effect and improvement as reasonably to promise the realization of his hopes, and no contemptible eminence in his art, before many years should have elapsed.

The even course of this cheering prosperity was, however, destined to experience a sudden and formidable interruption, and that, too, in a manner so strange and mysterious as to baffle all investigation, and throw upon the events themselves a shadow of almost supernatural horror.

Schalken had one evening remained in the master's studio considerably longer than his more volatile companions, who had gladly availed themselves of the excuse which the dusk of evening afforded, to withdraw from their several tasks, in order to finish a day of labour in the jollity and conviviality of the tavern. But Schalken worked for improvement, or rather for love. Besides, he was now engaged merely in sketching a design, an operation which, unlike that of colouring, might be continued as long as there was light sufficient to distinguish between canvas and charcoal. He had not then, nor, indeed, until long after, discovered the peculiar powers of his pencil, and he was engaged in composing a group of extremely roguish-looking and grotesque imps and demons, who were inflicting various ingenious torments upon a perspiring and pot-bellied St. Anthony, who reclined in the midst of them, apparently in the last stage of drunkenness. The young artist, however, though incapable of executing, or even of appreciating, anything of true sublimity, had, nevertheless, discernment enough to prevent his being by any means satisfied with his work; and many were the patient erasures and corrections which the limbs and features of saint and devil underwent, yet all without producing in their new arrangement anything of improvement or increased effect. The large, old-fashioned room was silent, and, with the exception of himself, quite deserted by its usual inmates. An hour had passed—nearly two-without any improved result. Daylight had already declined, and twilight was fast giving way to the darkness of night. The patience of the young man was exhausted, and he stood before his unfinished production, absorbed in no very pleasing ruminations, one hand buried in the folds of his long dark hair, and the other holding the piece of charcoal which had so ill executed its office, and which he now rubbed, without much regard to the sable streaks which it produced, with irritable pressure upon his ample Flemish inexpressibles.

"Pshaw!" said the young man aloud, "would that picture, devils, saint, and all, were where they should be-in hell!" A short, sudden laugh, uttered startlingly close to his ear,

instantly responded to the ejaculation. The artist turned
sharply round, and now for the first time became aware
that his labours had been overlooked by a stranger. Within
about a yard and a half, and rather behind him, there stood
what was, or appeared to be, the figure of an elderly man:
he wore a short cloak, and broad-brimmed hat, with a
conical crown, and in his hand, which was protected with
a heavy, gauntlet-shaped glove, he carried a long ebony
walking-stick, surmounted with what appeared, as it
glittered dimly in the twilight, to be a massive head of gold,
and upon the breast, through the folds of the cloak, there
shone what appeared to be the links of a rich chain of the
same metal. The room was so obscure that nothing further
of the appearance of the figure could be ascertained, and
the face was altogether overshadowed by the heavy flap of
the beaver which overhung it, so that not a feature could
be discerned. A quantity of dark hair escaped from beneath
this sombre hat, a circumstance which, connected with the
firm, upright carriage of the intruder, proved that his years
could not yet exceed threescore or thereabouts. There was an
air of gravity and importance about the garb of this person,
and something indescribably odd, I might say awful, in the
perfect stone-like movelessness of the figure, that effectually
checked the testy comment which had at once risen to the
lips of the irritated artist. He, therefore, as soon as he had

sufficiently recovered the surprise, asked the stranger, civilly, to be seated, and desired to know if he had any message to leave for his master.

"Tell Gerard Douw," said the unknown, without altering his attitude in the smallest degree, "that Minheer Vanderhausen, of Rotterdam, desires to speak with him on tomorrow evening at this hour, and, if he please, in this room, upon matters of weight—that is all—goodnight."

The stranger, having finished this message, turned abruptly, and with a quick but silent step quitted the room, before Schalken had time to say a word in reply. The young man felt a curiosity to see in what direction the burgher of Rotterdam would turn on quitting the studio, and for that purpose he went directly to the window which commanded the door. A lobby of considerable extent intervened between the inner door of the painter's room and the street entrance, so that Schalken occupied the post of observation before the old man could possibly have reached the street. He watched in vain, however. There was no other mode of exit. Had the old man vanished, or was he lurking about the recesses of the lobby for some bad purpose? This last suggestion filled the mind of Schalken with a vague horror, which was so unaccountably intense as to make him alike afraid to remain in the room alone and reluctant to pass through the lobby. However, with an effort which appeared very disproportioned to the occasion, he summoned resolution to leave the room, and, having double-locked the door and thrust the key in his pocket, without looking to the right or left, he traversed the passage which had so recently, perhaps still, contained the person of his mysterious visitant, scarcely venturing to breathe till he had arrived in the open street.

"Minheer Vanderhausen," said Gerard Douw within himself, as the appointed hour approached, "Minheer Vanderhausen of Rotterdam! I never heard of the man till yesterday. What can he want of me? A portrait, perhaps, to be painted; or a younger son or a poor relation to be apprenticed; or a collection to be valued; or—pshaw, there's no one in Rotterdam to leave me a legacy. Well, whatever the business may be, we shall soon know it all."

It was now the close of day, and every easel, except that of Schalken, was deserted. Gerald Douw was pacing the apartment with the restless step of impatient expectation, every now and then humming a passage from a piece of music which he was himself composing; for, though no great proficient, he admired the art: sometimes pausing to glance over the work of one of his absent pupils, but more frequently placing himself at the window, from whence he might observe the passengers who threaded the obscure bystreet, in which his studio was placed.

"Said you not, Godfrey," exclaimed Douw, after a long

and fruitless gaze from his post of observation, and turning to Schalken—"said you riot the hour of appointment was at about seven by the clock of the Stadhouse?"

"It had just tolled seven when I first saw him, sir," answered the student.

"The hour is close at hand, then," said the master, consulting a horologe as large and as round as a full-grown orange. "Minheer Vanderhausen from Rotterdam—is it not so?"

"Such was the name."

"And an elderly man, richly clad?" continued Douw.

"As well as I might see," replied his pupil; "he could not be young, nor yet very old neither, and his dress was rich and grave, as might become a citizen of wealth and consideration."

At this moment the sonorous boom of the Stadhouse clock tolled, stroke after stroke, the hour of seven; the eyes of both master and student were directed to the door; and it was not until the last peal of the old bell had ceased to vibrate, that Douw exclaimed:

"So, so; we shall have his worship presently—that is, if he means to keep his hour; if not, thou may'st wait for him, Godfrey, if you court the acquaintance of a capricious burgomaster; as for me, I think our old Leyden contains a sufficiency of such commodities, without an importation

13

from Rotterdam."

Schalken laughed, as in duty bound; and after a pause of some minutes, Douw suddenly exclaimed:

"What if it should all prove a jest, a piece of mummery got up by Vankarp, or some such worthy? I wish you had run all risks, and cudgelled the old burgomaster, stadholder, or whatever else he may be, soundly. I would wager a dozen of Rhenish, his worship would have pleaded old acquaintance before the third application."

"Here he comes, sir," said Schalken, in a low admonitory tone; and instantly upon turning towards the door, Gerard Douw observed the same figure which had, on the day before, so unexpectedly greeted the vision of his pupil Schalken.

There was something in the air and mein of the figure which at once satisfied the painter that there was no *mummery* in the case, and that he really stood in the presence of a man of worship; and so, without hesitation, he doffed his cap, and, courteously saluting the stranger, requested him to be seated. The visitor waved his hand slightly, as if in acknowledgement of the courtesy, but remained standing.

"I have the honour to see Minheer Vanderhausen of Rotterdam?" said Gerard Douw.

"The same," was the laconic reply of his visitant.

"I understand your worship desires to speak with me," continued Douw, "and I am here by appointment to wait your commands."

"Is that a man of trust?" said Vanderhausen, turning towards Schalken, who stood at a little distance behind his master.

"Certainly," replied Gerard.

"Then let him take this box and get the nearest jeweller or goldsmith to value its contents, and let him return hither with a certificate of the valuation."

At the same time, he placed a small case about nine inches square in the hands of Gerard Douw, who was as much amazed at its weight as at the strange abruptness with which it was handed to him. In accordance with the wishes of the stranger, he delivered it into the hands of Schalken, and repeating *his* directions, despatched him upon the mission.

Schalken disposed his precious charge securely beneath the folds of his cloak, and rapidly traversing two or three narrow streets, he stopped at a corner house, the lower part of which was then occupied by the shop of a Jewish goldsmith. Schalken entered the shop, and calling the little Hebrew into the obscurity of its back recesses, he proceeded to lay before him Vanderhausen's packet. On being examined by the light of a lamp, it appeared entirely cased with lead, the outer surface of which was much scraped and soiled, and nearly white with age. This was with difficulty partially removed and disclosed beneath a box of some dark and singularly hard wood; this too was forced, and after the removal of two or three folds of linen, its contents proved to be a mass of golden ingots, closely packed, and, as the Jew declared, of the most perfect quality. Every ingot underwent the scrutiny of the little Jew, who seemed to feel an epicurean delight in touching and testing these morsels of the glorious metal; and each one of them was replaced in its berth with the exclamation: "Mein Gott, how very perfect! Not one grain of alloy—beautiful, beautiful." The task was at length finished, and the Jew certified under his hand the value of the ingots submitted to his examination, to amount to many thousand rix-dollars. With the desired document in his bosom, and the rich box of gold carefully pressed under his arm, and concealed by his cloak, he retraced his way, and entering the studio, found his master and the stranger in close conference.

Schalken had no sooner left the room, in order to execute the commission he had taken in charge, than Vanderhausen addressed Gerard Douw in the following terms:

"I may not tarry with you tonight more than a few minutes, and so I shall briefly tell you the matter upon which I come. You visited the town of Rotterdam some four months ago, and then I saw in the church of St. Lawrence your niece, Rose Velderkaust. I desire to marry her, and if I satisfy you as to the fact that I am very wealthy, more wealthy than any husband you could dream of for her, I expect that you will forward my views to the utmost of your authority. If you approve my proposals, you must close with it at once, for I cannot command time enough to wait for calculations and delays."

Gerard Douw was, perhaps, as much astonished as any one could be, by the very unexpected nature of Minheer Vanderhausen's communication, but he did not give vent to any unseemly expression of surprise, for besides the motives supplied by prudence and politeness, the painter experienced a kind of chill and oppressive sensation, something like that which is supposed to affect a man who is placed unconsciously in immediate contact with something to which he has a natural antipathy—an undefined horror and dread while standing in the presence of the eccentric stranger, which made him very unwilling to say anything which might reasonably prove offensive.

"I have no doubt," said Gerard, after two or three prefatory hems, "that the connexion which you propose would prove alike advantageous and honourable to my niece; but you must be aware that she has a will of her own, and may not acquiesce in what *we* may desire for her advantage."

"Do not seek to deceive me, sir painter," said Vanderhausen; "you are her guardian—she is your ward—she is mine if *you* like to make her so."

The man of Rotterdam moved forward a little as he spoke, and Gerard Douw, he scarce knew why, inwardly prayed for the speedy return of Schalken.

"I desire," said the mysterious gentleman, "to place in your hands at once an evidence of my wealth, and a security for my liberal dealing with your niece. The lad will return in a minute or two with a sum in value five times the fortune which she has a right to expect from a husband. This shall lie in your hands, together with her dowry, and you may apply the united sum as suits her interest best; it shall be all exclusively hers while she lives—is that liberal?"

Douw assented, and inwardly thought that fortune had been extraordinarily kind to his niece; the stranger, he thought, must be both wealthy and generous, and such an offer was not to be despised, though made by a humorist, and one of no very prepossessing presence. Rose had no very high pretensions, for she was almost without dowry; indeed, altogether so, excepting so far as the deficiency had been supplied by the generosity of her uncle; neither had she any right to raise any scruples against the match on the score of birth, for her own origin was by no means elevated, and as to other objections, Gerard resolved, and, indeed, by the usages of the time, was warranted in resolving not to listen to them for a moment.

"Sir," said he, addressing the stranger, "your offer is most liberal, and whatever hesitation I may feel in closing with it immediately, arises solely from my not having the honour of knowing anything of your family or station. Upon these points you can, of course, satisfy me without difficulty?"

"As to my respectability," said the stranger, drily, "you must take that for granted at present; pester me with no inquiries; you can discover nothing more about me than I choose to make known. You shall have sufficient security for my respectability—my word, if you are honourable: if you are sordid, my gold."

"A testy old gentleman," thought Douw, "he must have his own way; but, all things considered, I am justified in giving my niece to him; were she my own daughter, I would do the like by her. I will not pledge myself unnecessarily however."

"You will not pledge yourself unnecessarily," said Vanderhausen, strangely uttering the very words which had just floated through the mind of his companion; "but you will do so if it *is* necessary, I presume; and I will show you that I consider it indispensable. If the gold I mean to leave in your hands satisfies you, and if you desire that my proposal shall not be at once withdrawn, you must, before I leave this room, write your name to this engagement."

Having thus spoken, he placed a paper in the hands of Gerard, the contents of which expressed an engagement entered into by Gerard Douw, to give to Wilken Vanderhausen of Rotterdam, in marriage, Rose Velderkaust, and so forth, within one week of the date thereof. While the painter was employed in reading this covenant, Schalken, as we have stated, entered the studio, and having delivered the box and the valuation of the Jew, into the hands of the stranger, he was about to retire, when Vanderhausen called to him to wait; and, presenting the case and the certificate to Gerard Douw, he waited in silence until he had satisfied himself by an inspection of both as to the value of the pledge left in his hands. At length he said:

"Are you content?"

The painter said he would fain have another day to consider.

"Not an hour," said the suitor coolly.

"Well then," said Douw, "I am content—it is a bargain."

"Then sign at once," said Vanderhausen, "I am weary."

At the same time he produced a small case of writing materials, and Gerard signed the important document.

"Let this youth sign the covenant," said the old man; and Godfrey Schalken unconsciously signed the instrument which bestowed upon another that hand which he had so long regarded as the object and reward of all his labours. The compact being thus completed, the strange visitor folded up the paper, and stowed it safely in an inner pocket.

"I will visit you tomorrow night at nine of the clock, at your house, Gerard Douw, and will see the subject of our contract—farewell"; and so saying, Wilken Vanderhausen moved stiffly but rapidly out of the room.

Schalken, eager to resolve his doubts, had placed himself by the window, in order to watch the street entrance; but the experiment served only to support his suspicions, for the old man did not issue from the door. This was very strange, very odd, very fearful; he and his master returned together, and talked but little on the way, for each had his own subjects for reflection, of anxiety, and of hope. Schalken, however, did not know the ruin which threatened his cherished schemes.

Gerard Douw knew nothing of the attachment which had sprung up between his pupil and his niece; and even if he had, it is doubtful whether he would have regarded its existence as any serious obstruction to the wishes of Minheer Vanderhausen. Marriages were then and there matters of traffic and calculation; and it would have appeared as absurd in the eyes of the guardian to make a mutual attachment an essential element in a contract of marriage, as it would have been to draw up his bonds and receipts in the language of chivalrous romance. The painter, however, did not communicate to his niece the important step which he had taken in her behalf, and his resolution arose not from any anticipation of opposition on her part, but solely from a ludicrous consciousness that if his ward were, as she very naturally might do, to ask him to describe the appearance of the bridegroom whom he destined for her, he would be forced to confess that he had not seen his face, and if called upon, would find it impossible to identify him. Upon the next day, Gerard Douw, having dined, called his niece to him and having scanned her person with an air of satisfaction, he took her hand, and looking upon her pretty, innocent face with a smile of kindness, he said:

"Rose, my girl, that face of yours will make your fortune." Rose blushed and smiled. "Such faces and such tempers seldom go together, and, when they do, the compound is a love potion, which few heads or hearts can resist; trust me, thou wilt soon be a bride, girl; but this is trifling, and I am pressed for time, so make ready the large room by eight o'clock tonight, and give directions for supper at nine. I expect a friend tonight; and observe me, child, do thou trick thyself out handsomely. I would not have him think us poor or sluttish."

With these words he left the chamber, and took his way to the room to which we have already had occasion to introduce our readers—that in which his pupils worked.

When the evening closed in, Gerard called Schalken, who was about to take his departure to his obscure and comfortless lodgings, and asked him to come home and sup with Rose and Vanderhausen. The invitation was, of course, accepted, and Gerard Douw and his pupil soon found themselves in the handsome and somewhat antique-looking room which had been prepared for the reception of the stranger. A cheerful wood fire blazed in the capacious health; a little at one side an old-fashioned table, with richly carved legs, was placed—destined, no doubt, to receive the supper, for which preparations were going forward; and ranged with exact regularity, stood the tall-backed chairs, whose un-gracefulness was more than counterbalanced by their comfort. The little party, consisting of Rose, her uncle, and the artist, awaited the arrival of the expected visitor with considerable impatience. Nine o'clock at length came, and with it a summons at the street door, which being speedily answered, was followed by a slow and emphatic tread upon the staircase; the steps moved heavily across the lobby, the door of the room in which the party which we have described were assembled slowly opened, and there entered a figure which startled, almost appalled, the phlegmatic Dutchman, and nearly made Rose scream with affright; it was the form, and arrayed in the garb of Minheer Vanderhausen; the air, the gait, the height were the same, but the features had never been seen by any of the party before. The stranger stopped at the door of the room, and displayed his form and face completely. He wore a dark-coloured cloth cloak, which was short and full, not falling quite to the knees; his legs were cased in dark purple silk stockings, and his shoes were adorned with roses of the same colour. The opening of the cloak in front showed the under-suit to consist of some very dark, perhaps sable material, and his hands were enclosed in a pair of heavy leather gloves, which ran up considerably above the wrist, in the manner of a gauntlet. In one hand he carried his walking-stick and his hat, which he had removed, and the other hung heavily by his side. A quantity of grizzled hair descended in long tresses from his head, arid its folds rested upon the plaits of a stiff ruff, which effectually concealed his neck. So far all was well; but the face!—all the flesh of the face was coloured with the bluish leaden hue which is sometimes produced by the operation of metallic medicines, administered in excessive quantities; the eyes were enormous, and the white appeared both above and below the iris, which gave to them an expression of insanity, which was heightened by their glassy fixedness; the nose was well enough, but the mouth was writhed considerably to one side, where it opened in order to give egress to two long, discoloured fangs, which projected from the upper jaw, far below the lower lip—the hue of the lips themselves bore the usual relation to that of the face, and was, consequently, nearly black; the character of the face was malignant, even satanic, to the last degree; and, indeed, such a combination of horror could hardly be accounted for, except by supposing the corpse of some atrocious malefactor which had long hung blackening upon the gibbet to have at length become the habitation of a demon—the frightful sport of satanic possession. It was remarkable that the worshipful stranger suffered as little as possible of his flesh to appear, and that during his visit he did not once remove his gloves. Having stood for some moments at the door, Gerard Douw at length found breath and collectedness to bid him welcome, and with a mute inclination of the head, the stranger stepped forward into the room. There was something indescribably odd, even horrible, about all his motions, something indefinable, that was unnatural, un-human—it was as if the limbs were guided and directed by a spirit unused to the management of bodily machinery. The stranger said hardly anything during his visit, which did not exceed half an hour; and the host himself could scarcely muster courage enough to utter the few necessary salutations and courtesies; and, indeed, such was the nervous terror which the presence of Vanderhausen inspired, that very little would have made all his entertainers fly bellowing from the room. They had not so far lost all self-possession, however, as to fail to observe two strange peculiarities of their visitor. During his stay he did not once suffer his eyelids to close, nor even to move in the slightest degree; and farther, there was a death-like stillness in his whole person, owing to the total absence of the heaving motion of the chest, caused by the process of respiration. These two peculiarities, though when told they may appear trifling, produced a very striking and unpleasant effect when seen and observed. Vanderhausen at length relieved the painter of. Leyden of his inauspicious presence; and with no small gratification the little party heard the street door close after him.

"Dear uncle," said Rose, "what a frightful man! I would not see him again for the wealth of the States."

"Tush, foolish girl," said Douw, whose sensations were anything but comfortable. "A man may be as ugly as the devil, and yet if his heart and actions are good, he is worth all the pretty-faced, perfumed puppies that walk the Mall. Rose, my girl, it is very true he has not thy pretty face, but I know him to be wealthy and liberal; and were he ten times more ugly"—("which is inconceivable," observed Rose)— "these two virtues would be sufficient," continued her uncle, "to counter-balance all his deformity, and if not of power sufficient actually to alter the shape of the features, at least of efficacy enough to prevent one thinking them amiss."

"Do you know, uncle," said Rose, "when I saw him standing at the door, I could not get it out of my head that I saw the old, painted, wooden figure that used to frighten me so much in the church of St. Lawrence of Rotterdam."

Gerard laughed, though he could not help inwardly acknowledging the justness of the comparison. He was resolved, however, as far as he could, to check his niece's inclination to ridicule the ugliness of her intended bridegroom, although he was not a little pleased to observe that she appeared totally exempt from that mysterious dread of the stranger which, he could not disguise it from himself, considerably affected him, as also his pupil Godfrey Schalken.

Early on the next day there arrived from various quarters of the town, rich presents of silks, velvets, jewellery, and so forth, for Rose; and also a packet directed to Gerard Douw, which on being opened, was found to contain a contract of marriage, formally drawn up, between Wilken Vanderhausen of the Boom-quay, in Rotterdam, and Rose Velderkaust, of Leyden, niece to Gerard Douw, master in the art of painting, also of the same city; and containing engagements on the part of Vanderhausen to make settlements upon his bride, far more splendid than he had before led her guardian to believe likely, and which were to be secured to her use in the most unexceptionable. manner possible—the money being placed in the hands of Gerard Douw himself.

I have no sentimental scenes to describe, no cruelty of guardians, or magnanimity of wards, or agonies of lovers. The record I have to make is one of sordidness, levity, and interest. In less than a week after the first interview which we have just described, the contract of marriage was fulfilled, and Schalken saw the prize which he would have risked anything to secure, carried off triumphantly by his unattractive rival. For two or three days he absented himself from the school; he then returned and worked, if with less cheerfulness, with far more dogged resolution than before—the stimulus of love had given place to that of ambition. Months passed away, and, contrary to his expectation, and, indeed, to the direct promise of the parties, Gerard Douw heard nothing of his niece or her worshipful spouse. The interest of the money which was to have been demanded in quarterly sums, lay unclaimed in his hands. He began to grow extremely uneasy. Minheer Vanderhausen's direction in Rotterdam he was fully possessed of; after some irresolution he finally determined to journey thither—a trifling undertaking, and easily accomplished—and thus to satisfy himself of the safety and comfort of his ward, for whom he entertained an honest and strong affection. His search was in vain, however; no one in Rotterdam had ever heard of Minheer Vanderhausen. Gerard Douw left not a house in the Boom-quay untried; but all in vain—no one could give him any information whatever touching the object of his inquiry; and he was obliged to return to Leyden nothing wiser than when he had left it. On his arrival he hastened to the establishment from which

Vanderhausen had hired the lumbering, though, considering the times, most luxurious vehicle, which the bridal party had employed to convey them to Rotterdam. From the driver of this machine he learned, that having proceeded by slow stages, they had late in the evening approached Rotterdam; but that before they entered the city, and while yet nearly a mile from it, a small party of men, soberly clad, and after the old fashion, with peaked beards and moustaches, standing in the centre of the road, obstructed the further progress of the carriage. The driver reined in his horses, much fearing, from the obscurity of the hour, and the loneliness of the road, that some mischief was intended. His fears were, however, somewhat allayed by his, observing that these strange men carried a large litter, of an antique shape, and which they immediately set down upon the pavement, whereupon the bridegroom, having opened the coach-door from within, descended, and having assisted his bride to do likewise, led her, weeping bitterly and wringing her hands, to the litter, which they both entered. It was then raised by the men who surrounded it, and speedily carried towards the city, and before it had proceeded many yards, the darkness concealed it from the view of the Dutch charioteer. In the inside of the vehicle he found a purse, whose contents more than thrice paid the hire of the carriage and man. He saw and could tell nothing more of Minheer Vandehausen and his beautiful lady. This mystery was a source of deep anxiety and almost of grief to Gerard Douw. There was evidently fraud in the dealing of Vanderhausen with him, though for what purpose committed he could not imagine. He greatly doubted how far it was possible for a man possessing in his countenance so strong an evidence of the presence of the most demoniac feelings, to be in reality anything but a villain, and every day that passed without his hearing from or of his niece, instead of inducing him to forget his fears, on the contrary tended more and more to exasperate them. The loss of his niece's cheerful society tended also to depress his spirits; and in order to dispel this despondency, which often crept upon his mind after his daily employment was over, he was wont frequently to prevail upon Schalken to accompany him home, and by his presence to dispel, in some degree, the gloom of his otherwise solitary supper. One evening, the painter and his pupil were sitting by the fire, having accomplished a comfortable supper, and had yielded \to that silent pensiveness sometimes induced by the process of digestion, when their reflections were disturbed by a loud sound at the street door, as if occasioned by some person rushing forcibly and repeatedly against it. A domestic had run without delay to ascertain the cause of the disturbance, and they heard him twce or thrice interrogate the applicant for admission, but without producing an answer or any cessation of the sounds. They heard him then open the hall door, and immediately there followed a light and rapid tread upon the staircase. Schalken laid his hand on his sword, and advanced towards the door. It opened before he reached it, and Rose rushed into the room. She looked wild and haggard, and pale with exhaustion and terror, but her dress surprised them as much as even her unexpected appearance. It consisted of a kind of white woollen wrapper, made close about the neck, and descending to the very ground. It was much deranged and travel-soiled. The poor creature had hardly entered the chamber when she fell senseless on the floor. With some difficulty they succeeded in reviving her, and on recovering her senses, she instantly exclaimed, in a tone of eager, terrified impatience:

"Wine, wine, quickly, or I'm lost."

Much alarmed at the strange agitation in which the call was made, they at once administered to her wishes, and she drank some wine with a haste and eagerness which surprised them. She had hardly swallowed it, when she exclaimed, with the same urgency:

"Food, food, at once, or I perish."

A considerable fragment of a roast joint was upon the table, and Schalken immediately proceeded to cut some, but he was anticipated, for no sooner had she become aware of its presence, than she darted at it with the rapacity of a vulture, and, seizing it in her hands, she tore off the flesh with her teeth, and swallowed it. When the paroxysm of hunger had been a little appeased, she appeared suddenly to become aware how strange her conduct had been, or it may have been that other more agitating thoughts recurred to her mind, for she began to weep bitterly and to wring her hands.

"Oh, send for a minister of God," said she; "I am not safe till he comes; send for him speedily."

Gerard Douw despatched a messenger instantly, and prevailed on his niece to allow him to surrender his bedchamber to her use; he also persuaded her to retire to it at once and to rest; her consent was extorted upon the condition that they would not leave her for a moment.

"Oh that the holy man were here," she said; "he can deliver me—the dead and the living can never be one—God has forbidden it."

With these mysterious words she surrendered herself to their guidance, and they proceeded to the chamber which Gerard Douw had assigned to her use.

"Do not, do not leave me for a moment," said she; "I am lost for ever if you do."

Gerard Douw's chamber was approached through a spacious apartment, which they were now about to enter. Gerard Douw and Schalken each carried a wax candle, so that a sufficient degree of light was cast upon all surrounding objects. They were now entering the large chamber, which, as I have said, communicated with Douw's apartment, when Rose suddenly stopped, and, in a whisper which seemed to thrill with horror, she said:

"Oh, God! he is here, he is here; see, see, there he goes."

She pointed towards the door of the inner room, and Schalken thought he saw a shadowy and ill-defined form gliding into that apartment. He drew his sword, and, raising the candle so as to throw its light with increased distinctness upon the objects in the room, he entered the chamber into which the shadow had glided. No figure was there—nothing but the furniture which belonged to the room, and yet he could not be deceived as to the fact that something had moved before them into the chamber. A sickening dread came upon him, and the cold perspiration broke' out in heavy drops upon his forehead; nor was he more composed, when he heard the increased urgency, the agony of entreaty, with which Rose implored them not to leave her for a moment.

"I saw him," said she; "he's here. I cannot be deceived—I know him—he's by me—he is with me—he's in the room; then, for God's sake, as you would save me, do not stir from beside me."

They at length prevailed upon her to lie down upon the bed, where she continued to urge them to stay by her. She frequently uttered incoherent sentences, repeating, again and again, "the dead and the living cannot be one—God has forbidden it"; and then again, "rest to the wakeful—sleep to the sleep-walkers". These and such mysterious and broken sentences, she continued to utter until the clergyman arrived. Gerard Douw began to fear, naturally enough, that the poor girl, owing to terror or ill-treatment, had become deranged, and he half-suspected, by the suddenness of her appearance, and the unseasonableness of the hour, and, above all, from the wildness and terror of her manner, that she had made her escape from some place of confinement for lunatics, and was in immediate fear of pursuit. He resolved to summon medical advice, as soon as the mind of his niece had been in some measure set at rest by the offices of the clergyman whose attendance she had so earnestly desired; and until this object had been attained, he did not venture to put any questions to her which might possibly, by reviving painful or horrible recollections, increase her agitation. The clergyman soon arrived—a man of ascetic countenance and venerable age—one whom Gerard Douw respected much, forasmuch as he was a veteran polemic, though one, perhaps, more dreaded as a combatant than beloved as a Christian—of pure morality, subtle brain, and frozen heart. He entered the chamber which communicated with that in which Rose reclined, and immediately on his arrival, she requested him to pray for her, as for one who lay in the hands of Satan, and who could hope for deliverance-only from heaven.

That our readers may distinctly understand all the circumstances of the event which we are about imperfectly to describe, it is necessary to state the relative positions of the parties who were engaged in it. The old clergyman and Schalken were in the ante-room of which we have already spoken; Rose lay in the inner chamber, the door of which was open; and by the side of the bed, at her urgent desire, stood her guardian; a candle burned in the bedchamber, and three were lighted in the outer apartment. The old man now cleared his voice as if about to commence, but before he had time to begin, a sudden gust of air blew out the candle which served to illuminate the room in which the poor girl lay, and she, with hurried alarm, exclaimed:

"Godfrey, bring in another candle; the darkness is unsafe."

Gerard Douw, forgetting for the moment her repeated injunctions, in the immediate impulse, stepped from the bedchamber into the other, in order to supply what she desired.

"Oh God! do not go, dear uncle," shrieked the unhappy girl—and at the same time she sprang from the bed, and darted after him, in order, by her grasp, to detain him. But the warning came too late, for scarcely had he passed the threshold, and hardly had his niece had time to utter the startling exclamation, when the door which divided the two rooms closed violently after him, as if swung to by a strong blast of wind. Schalken and he both rushed to the door, but their united and desperate efforts could not avail so much as to shake it. Shriek after shriek burst from the inner chamber, with all the piercing loudness of despairing terror-. Schalken and Douw applied every energy and strained every nerve to force open the door; but all in vain. There was no sound of struggling from within, but the screams seemed to increase in loudness, and at the same time they heard the bolts of the latticed window withdrawn, and the window itself grated upon the sill as if thrown open. One *last* shriek, so long and piercing and agonized as to be scarcely human, swelled from the room, and suddenly there followed a death-like silence. A light step was heard crossing the floor, as if from the bed to the window; and almost at the same instant the door gave way, and, yielding to the pressure of the external applicants, they were nearly precipitated into the room. It was empty. The window was open, and Schalken sprang to a chair and gazed out upon the street and canal below. He saw no form, but he beheld, or thought he beheld, the waters of the broad canal beneath settling ring after ring in heavy circular ripples, as if a moment before disturbed by the immersion of some large and heavy mass.

No trace of Rose was ever after discovered, nor was anything certain respecting her mysterious wooer detected or even suspected—no clue whereby to trace the intricacies of the labyrinth and to arrive at a distinct conclusion was to be found. But an incident occurred which, though it will not be received by our rational readers as at all approaching to evidence upon the matter, nevertheless produced a strong and a lasting impression upon the mind of Schalken. Many years after the events which we have detailed, Schalken, then remotely situated, received an intimation of his father's death, and of his intended burial upon a fixed day in the church of Rotterdam. It was necessary that a very considerable journey should be performed by the funeral procession, which, as it will be readily believed, was not very numerously attended. Schalken with difficulty arrived in Rotterdam late in the day upon which the funeral was appointed to take place. It had not then arrived. Evening closed in, and still it did not appear.

Schalken strolled down to the church—he found it open—notice of the arrival of the. funeral had been given, and the vault in which the body was to be laid had been opened. The officer, who is analogous to our sexton, on seeing a well-dressed gentleman, whose object was to attend the expected funeral, pacing the aisle of the church, hospitably invited him to share with him the comforts of a blazing wood fire, which, as was his custom in winter time upon such occasions, he had kindled in the hearth of a chamber which communicated, by a flight of steps, with the vault below. In this chamber Schalken and his entertainer seated themselves, and the sexton, after some fruitless attempts to engage his guest in conversation, was obliged to apply himself to his tobacco-pipe and can, to solace his solitude. In spite of his grief and cares, the fatigues of a rapid journey of nearly forty hours gradually overcame the mind and body of Godfrey Schalken and he sank into a deep sleep, from which he was awakened by someone's shaking him gently by the shoulder. He first thought that the old sexton had called him, but *he* was no longer in the room. He roused himself, and as soon as he could clearly see what was around him, he perceived a female form, clothed in a kind of light robe of muslin, part of which was so disposed as to act as a veil, and in her hand she carried a lamp. She was moving rather away from him and towards the flight of steps which conducted towards the vaults. Schalken felt a vague alarm at the sight of this figure, and at the same time an irresistible impulse to follow its guidance. He followed it towards the vaults, but when it reached the head of the stairs, he paused—the figure paused also, and, turning gently round, displayed, by the light of the lamp it carried, the face and features of his first love, Rose Velderkaust. There was nothing horrible, or even sad, in the countenance. On the contrary, it wore the same arch smile which used to enchant the artist long before in his happy days. A feeling of awe and of interest, too intense to be resisted, prompted him to follow the spectre, if spectre it were. She descended the stairs—he followed— and, turning to the left, through a narrow passage, she led him, to his infinite surprise, into what appeared to be an old-fashioned Dutch apartment, such as the pictures of Gerard Douw have served to immortalize. Abundance of costly antique furniture was disposed about the room, and in one corner stood a four-post bed, with heavy black cloth curtains around it; the figure frequently turned towards him with the same arch smile; and when she came to the side of the bed, she drew the curtains, and, by the light of the lamp, which she held towards its contents, she disclosed to the horror-stricken painter, sitting bolt upright in bed, the livid and demoniac form of Vanderhausen. Schalken had hardly seen him, when he fell senseless upon the floor, where he lay until discovered, on the next morning, by persons employed in closing the passages into the vaults. He was lying in a cell of considerable size, which had not been disturbed for a long time, and he had fallen beside a large coffin, which was supported upon small stone pillars, a security against the attacks of vermin.

To his dying day Schalken was satisfied of the reality of the vision which he had witnessed, and he has left behind him a curious evidence of the impression which it wrought upon his fancy, in a painting executed shortly after the event we have narrated, and which is valuable as exhibiting not only the peculiarities which have made Schalken's pictures sought after, but even more so as presenting a portrait as close and faithful as one taken from memory can be, of his early love, Rose Velderkaust, whose mysterious fate must ever remain a matter of speculation. The picture represents a chamber of antique masonry, such as might be found in most old cathedrals, and is lighted faintly by a lamp carried in the hand of a female figure, such as we have above attempted to describe; and in the background, and to the left of him who examines the painting, there stands the form of a man apparently aroused from sleep, and by his attitude, his hand being laid upon his sword, exhibiting considerable alarm; this last figure is illuminated only by the expiring glare of a wood or charcoal fire. The whole production exhibits a beautiful specimen of that artful and singular distribution of light and shade which has rendered the name of Schalken immortal among the artists of his country. This tale is traditionary, and the reader will easily perceive by our studiously omitting to heighten many points of the narrative, when a little additional colouring might have added effect to the recital, that we have desired to lay before him, not a figment of the brain, but a curious tradition connected with, and belonging to, the biography of a famous artist.

www.ingramcontent.com/pod-product-compliance
Lightning Source LLC
Chambersburg PA
CBHW030543180626
46810CB00005B/1985